# THE BLACKBELT CLUB

# Night on the Mountain of Fear

D0103947

*The dojo at Karate Kids World*

# THE BLACK BELT CLUB

# Night on the Mountain of Fear

## DAWN BARNES

### illustrated by
### BERNARD CHANG

## THE BLUE SKY PRESS
An Imprint of Scholastic Inc. • New York

THE BLUE SKY PRESS

Text copyright © 2006 by Dawn Barnes
Illustrations copyright © 2006 by Dawn Barnes
All rights reserved.

Special thanks to Robert Martin Staenberg.

Thank you to Ms. Lisa Bartoli and her fourth-grade class
for their detailed comments about this manuscript.

SCHOLASTIC, THE BLUE SKY PRESS, and associated logos
are trademarks and/or registered trademarks of Scholastic Inc.

Library of Congress catalog card number: 2005004572

ISBN 0-439-63939-5

12 11 10 9 8 7 6 5 4 3 2 1      6 7 8 9 10/0
Printed in the United States of America      40

First printing, September 2006

*For my friends—who remind me that love is*

*the most powerful force in the universe*

*— D.B.*

*For my father, Martin.*

*With special thanks to Bonnie, Dawn, Kathleen,*

*Anamika, and Emmy.*

*— B.C.*

# CHAPTER 1

EXCITEMENT FILLED the dojo. It was Saturday morning, and Karate Kids World was packed with students and parents watching the ultimate Black Belt Club challenge—a contest to see who could remember twenty moves in a row without stopping. And the students didn't even know what the moves were ahead of time!

"Kick! Punch! Roll! Jump up! Drop and spin!" commanded Sensei.

*"Osu!"* we yelled, to show we understood.

Being part of the Black Belt Club was hard work! Everyone was ahead of me, as usual.

Right now, there are still just four of us in the Black Belt Club: me, Maia, Jamie, and Antonio. Sensei calls us the Champions of the Four Winds. Today we are the demo team. We do the moves, and the other kids try to copy what we do.

Sensei says she wants to train a few more students for a future invitation into the club. I hope she's not thinking about replacing any of us. If she does, I'll probably be the first. I mean, everyone knows that Maia's the smartest, Jamie's the best at teamwork, and Antonio's the bravest. But I'm the one who worries the most.

Thirty students showed up today to try out. Even though they're already black belts, they're going to have to be *really* good to get invited into the Black Belt Club. You never know, though. I mean, *I* made it, and I know the other kids all wondered why — especially Maia. I can tell she thinks Sensei made a mistake.

Now, in the dojo, Antonio was doubled over on the mat, with Maia standing above him.

"Oh!" yelled the crowd.

ARE YOU *OKAY*?

I DID THE MOVE *CORRECTLY*.

HE'S THE ONE WHO DIDN'T HAVE HIS *GUARD* UP.

YES, BUT IT'S UP TO EACH OF YOU TO MAINTAIN *CONTROL* AND USE *LIGHT* CONTACT. RIGHT, MAIA?

*OSU, SENSEI!*

Antonio slowly got up to his feet. The audience applauded. Everyone's parents came to watch the contest. My father was away in China, so I'd asked my Uncle Al to come. I didn't see him though. He was always late — that is, if he came at all.

"Max!" Sensei called.

I jumped out of my daze.

"You're up!"

"*Osu*, Sensei!" I yelled, and I sprinted to the middle of the mat.

*Oh boy, everyone's watching. I thought we were going to demonstrate as a team! I guess not. I hate this part, but Sensei told me that I have to be a role model for the other kids at the dojo. But I usually mess up when too many people are looking at me.*

My mind was racing. *How did I ever get picked for the Black Belt Club? Maia never makes a mistake, so I know why she's in the club. Antonio is really fast and strong, so it makes sense that he's in the club. And Jamie helps Sensei a lot in the classes for the younger kids. She's already like a junior sensei. But why me?*

*Uncle Al says I can't do anything right. But when I told that to Sensei, she said I can do lots of things right, and that I earned my place in the Black Belt Club. I proved myself on our last mission. Sensei even called me a hero. Still . . .*

JUMPING FRONT KICK, LANDING IN A READY STANCE WITH A JAB-REVERSE PUNCH...

FOLLOWED BY A HOPPING SIDE KICK AND BACK KNUCKLE STRIKE. THEN DO TWO PIVOTING SIDE KICKS...

A SPINNING HOOK KICK, A SHOULDER ROLL, AND FLIP ONTO YOUR HANDS AND KNEES.

FINISH ON THE GROUND WITH A DOUBLE MULE KICK.

'KIAI' ON EVERY MOVE.

I glanced around the room, but I still didn't see Uncle Al. Jamie gave me a thumbs-up. My stomach was churning. My eyes darted back and forth. *So many people!*

"Go, Max!" yelled one of the little kids. Then, some other kids yelled, too. Pretty soon they were all yelling, "Go, Max!"

*OK, I can do it . . . I think. I've got to use my* ki *power. Sensei says my* ki *is my spirit power inside of me. Here goes.*

I jerked my back knee forward and up into the air, to give myself a lift. Then my front leg swung up to complete my jumping front kick. For a split second, I felt as if I were flying. It was great! I love jump kicks. They're the most fun of all the karate moves I know. Super frog power! Lost in my thoughts, the ground came up fast. It was a crash landing!

There I was, Max Greene, a member of the elite Black Belt Club, lying flat on my back. *What a role model!* I wished there had been a hole in the mat that I could have crawled into.

"Jump up, Max! Let's go!" commanded Sensei.

I couldn't move. I felt like a brick of cement. Some of the kids began laughing.

Maia shook her head and rolled her eyes at me. The competition continued. Now there were only ten kids left out of thirty. These were some of the best karate kids in the dojo. They jumped, spun, and kicked their way back and forth across the mat. Sensei kept a scorecard on each student.

It was time for the final contest. All the kids were nervous, but I think their parents were even more nervous. I sat in the corner, next to the special cupboard—the one that holds the Box of the Four Doors. A quiet ring sounded from behind the doors. *Chimes!* I knew what that meant. I went over to Sensei and whispered in her ear.

She clapped her hands, and instantly the final ten students stopped.

KARATE KIDS, YOU ARE ALL EXTREMELY TALENTED. I AM GOING TO NEED MORE TIME TO EVALUATE YOU TO MAKE MY DECISION.

BECAUSE OF YOUR EXCELLENT PERFORMANCES TODAY, THE FINALISTS WILL EACH RECEIVE A MEDAL OF ACHIEVEMENT TO TAKE HOME.

YEAH!

THEN, NEXT WEEK, I WILL CONTINUE WATCHING ALL OF YOU IN YOUR REGULAR CLASSES. TO BE IN THE *BLACK BELT CLUB*, YOU MUST DEMONSTRATE EXCELLENCE IN *MIND*, *BODY*, AND *SPIRIT*--BALANCE AT SCHOOL, THE DOJO, AND AT HOME.

YOU MUST SHOW KINDNESS AND LEADERSHIP, AND MOST OF ALL, YOU MUST TRY TO MAKE THE WORLD A BETTER PLACE. THIS IS THE PRIMARY CODE OF A *BLACK BELT CLUB* MEMBER.

We helped Sensei hand out the medals, and everyone left happy.

When the dojo was cleared, the chimes rang again in the cupboard.

*CHAMPIONS OF THE FOUR WINDS*, YOU ARE BEING CALLED ON A MISSION. GO HOME, EAT A HEALTHY MEAL, AND PREPARE. MEET BACK HERE AT TWO O'CLOCK THIS AFTERNOON. DON'T BE LATE.

*Not again,* I thought. Last time we had a "special workshop," I was knee-deep in slimy things, and I almost got eaten alive.

We bowed and left the dojo. The others went out and met their parents, who were waiting for them in the lobby. Uncle Al still hadn't shown up, so I ran outside alone to catch the bus.

# CHAPTER 2

I WONDER if there's any chance that Dad's back from China yet? Probably not, or he would have come to watch me today. Uncle Al lives with us and takes care of me when Dad's out of town, which is most of the time. We live in a small house, just off the freeway. The cars are really noisy, so when I'm trying to go to sleep, I pretend there's a rushing river outside my window. I like to imagine things like that.

I opened the front door. Uncle Al was sitting in his favorite chair in front of the television. "Close the door!" he yelled. "I've got the air-conditioning on."

Lucy came running full speed and jumped into my arms. She's a mutt and loves to lick my face. I think she's mostly French bulldog because of her ears. She gets really excited to see me because I play games with her and I've been training her.

STOP PLAYING WITH THE DOG. YOU'RE MAKING HER *HYPER!* WHERE WERE YOU, ANYWAY?

I WAS ON THE DEMO TEAM FOR THE *BLACK BELT CLUB* TODAY, REMEMBER? I TOLD YOU ABOUT IT.

I carried Lucy to my bedroom and closed the door. I sat on the floor. She jumped on me and wagged her tail. She always knows when I'm sad. Uncle Al *never* knows. Or if he does know, he doesn't care.

Lucy helped me clean the kitchen. She licked the floor and the plates inside the dishwasher. I was almost finished, and it was one-thirty.

"Uncle Al, could you give me a ride to the dojo?"

"Do I look like a taxi service?" He inspected the kitchen. "All right, looks clean. You can go, but don't be home late!"

"OK."

He stepped forward. *He's going to give me a hug!* But he grabbed Lucy instead.

GET GOING. YOU'LL MISS THE BUS.

# CHAPTER 3

WHEN WE all got to the dojo, we sat in a circle around the Box of the Four Doors. It feels really special to be here, because only the BBC gets to do this — it's our secret. Sensei opened the acorn-shaped lid and revealed five large crystals.

"To begin your journey, you must each call upon your Animal Power. Use these sacred stones to help you," said Sensei.

We each chose a crystal and held it up over the box. They shone in different colors as sunlight from the window streamed through them. I closed my eyes and concentrated on my Animal Power.

I felt my crystal getting warmer in my hand, and I opened my eyes. Glowing within it was a big bear showing his sharp teeth. *Yes! I did it!*

I looked at Maia and saw the crane in her stone. Jamie's eagle flew upon an invisible breeze inside her crystal. Antonio's Animal Power is the bull. That's such a perfect power for him because he's always charging ahead of everyone else.

We held our stones together over the center of the circle.

NORTH, SOUTH, EAST, AND WEST-- WE WILL ALWAYS TRY OUR BEST!

The box began to spin—slowly at first, then faster and faster. Just when I thought it would blast into the air, it stopped.

The West door flipped open. Standing before us was a glowing hologram of a woman who looked something like a picture I'd once seen of a Native American elder. Her long white hair blew in a gentle wind. Her red cloak was woven from a blanket. She lifted her hands to the sky and spoke.

AHO! I AM *GRANDMOTHER DANCING FEATHER.*

"Hato is a powerful opponent," said Sensei.

"It is the enemy of love," the elder continued. "The Hate Master will do everything he can to make you afraid. You must be swift, brave warriors."

Her hologram faded, and the box was silent.

IT'S A MISSION! TIME FOR THE *FOUR WINDS KATA!*

"But the rules are that you must *all* agree to go," Sensei reminded Antonio.

"Does everyone have to go?" asked Maia. She gave me a sideways glance.

"Of course," Sensei answered. "Only together are you the Champions."

"But shouldn't we take a vote?" I asked.

Out of the corner of my eye I saw Maia flap her elbows like wings. *I know she thinks I'm a chicken.*

"You're right, Max," answered Sensei. "You always have a choice here. Everyone who wants to go, raise your hand."

We all did—even me. I glared at Maia. She looked surprised.

"Good! Then move into position," said Sensei. "Each of you will certainly need your full Animal Power today."

We took our places for the Four Winds Kata. Maia bumped my shoulder as she passed by me.

I stood across from her and closed my eyes. *I'm going to really get my bear power today so I can do the best kata ever. Better than anyone here.* I peeked and saw Maia balancing on one leg, graceful as her crane.

I closed my eyes again and concentrated. From deep inside my mind, my bear showed itself. It ran to me from far away. As he came closer, I could feel his strength inside my body. I was ready. I opened my eyes and began my kata. At the same time, Jamie moved as an eagle, her arms gliding on the wind, while her eyes focused on a distant place. Antonio threw punches and jabs, like the thrusting horns of a charging bull.

Our kata began slowly at first and then sped up as our power grew. I could feel the magic moment approaching—the moment when we moved together in perfect balance, rhythm, and timing.

KIAI!

And in a flash of wind and light, we were gone.

# CHAPTER 4

WE DANCED our kata at high speed. Then we began to slow down, until we finally stopped.

We stood on a stone ledge projecting from a mountainside, high above the ground. We looked out across the valley and saw canyons and desert. Then we turned to face the mountain. To our amazement, we stood next to ten cliff houses, carved directly into the mountain. They were stacked on top of each other like an apartment building made of stone. Every house was dark inside except for the middle one. Candlelight shone from its windows and doorway.

"Let's check it out," said Antonio.

*He is always the one to lead the way. I wish I could be as brave as he is.*

We cautiously walked through the door and entered a large living room. The stone walls were decorated with masks and all kinds of animal parts: fur, skulls, feathers, and bones.

THIS IS **CREEPY**. WHY ARE DEAD THINGS EVERYWHERE?

Colorful rugs and blankets covered the floor. Antonio walked over to a table and picked up a pair of painted rattles. The handles were wrapped with red leather ties.

"Ah!" screamed Antonio, throwing the rattles. They had suddenly transformed into giant cockroaches! The cockroaches ran circles around his feet. Antonio looked as if he were tap dancing.

"Get away from me!" he shouted. They ran across his shoe and scurried out the door.

*Not more homework,* I thought. *I've got too much already.*

Grandmother answered as if she had heard me. "In our world, knowledge is power, so let me help you get some."

"Yes, ma'am," I said.

EVERYONE, COME HERE AND SIT IN A CIRCLE. IT'S TIME TO MAKE YOUR *PROTECTION POUCHES.*

BUT WE'RE THE *BLACK BELT CLUB.* WE CAN PROTECT OURSELVES.

*I'll take extra protection!* I thought.

"You may know karate, but you will need some different tools for the spirit world."

*Spirits? As in, people with no bodies?*

She set four baskets down in front of us. The first one held four deerskin pouches that had been dyed different colors: red, yellow, black, and white.

Reaching into the second basket, Jamie held up a strand of blue glass beads. I looked into the third.

THESE BEADS ARE BEAUTIFUL, GRANDMOTHER.

ARE THOSE REAL?

GROSS!

THE TOOTH OF A *MOUNTAIN LION* GIVES YOU COURAGE.

"I'll stick with the geodes," said Maia. From the fourth basket, she picked up a shiny yellow citrine stone.

NOW, EVERYONE CHOOSE A *POUCH*.

I picked the white one, and Maia took yellow.

"Black for me," said Jamie.

"Red, for power and energy!" said Antonio.

"Good," said Grandmother. "Your color will be the direction you must serve on this mission." She opened a small bag, and a strong smell came out.

Grandmother took a pinch of smudge between her fingers, and she sprinkled some into each of our pouches.

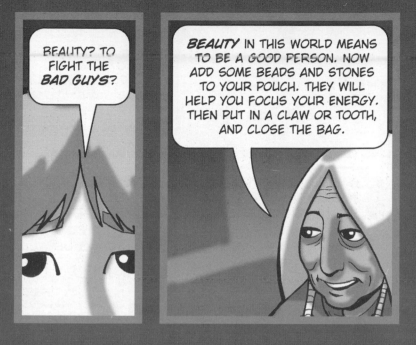

She picked up a stick and began beating her drum. *Boom-boom, boom-boom, boom-boom!* She drummed steadily, and I could feel the sound vibrating in my body.

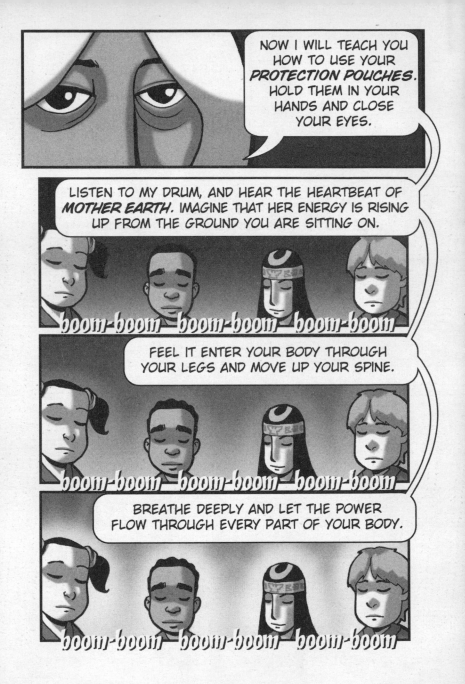

NOW I WILL TEACH YOU HOW TO USE YOUR *PROTECTION POUCHES.* HOLD THEM IN YOUR HANDS AND CLOSE YOUR EYES.

LISTEN TO MY DRUM, AND HEAR THE HEARTBEAT OF *MOTHER EARTH.* IMAGINE THAT HER ENERGY IS RISING UP FROM THE GROUND YOU ARE SITTING ON.

*boom-boom boom-boom boom-boom*

FEEL IT ENTER YOUR BODY THROUGH YOUR LEGS AND MOVE UP YOUR SPINE.

*boom-boom boom-boom boom-boom*

BREATHE DEEPLY AND LET THE POWER FLOW THROUGH EVERY PART OF YOUR BODY.

*boom-boom boom-boom boom-boom*

I concentrated on Grandmother's words and noticed that my hands began to tingle as if sparks of electricity were moving through them. Then my arms and legs began to shake a little. *I feel as if I could do a million jumping jacks right now!*

ONCE YOU FEEL THE VIBRATION MOVING THROUGH YOUR BODY, LET IT POUR OUT OF YOUR SKIN.

*Is something going to leak out of me?* I opened one eye and peeked at my arm.

"Wow!" I said with a start. The others opened their eyes, too. We were each surrounded by a bright ball of light.

Jamie and Maia stood up, and their balls of energy went with them. Maia began moving her arms around in a slow-motion kata, kind of like tai chi. "So, this ball of energy moves when we move?" she asked.

"Yes, as long as you keep focusing on pulling energy up from Mother Earth," Grandmother answered.

*Boom! Boom! Boom!* She gave the drum three final pounds with her stick and suddenly stopped. We turned to her, startled, and our balls of energy faded away.

She passed around four wooden hoops and some leather ties.

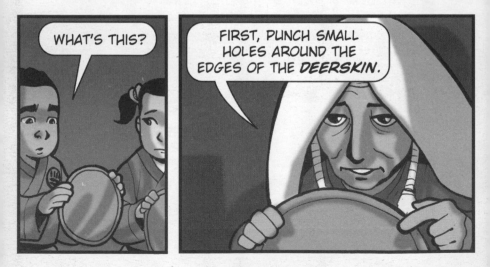

We did as she told us and held up our blank shields.

"What are these things supposed to do, anyway?" asked Antonio. "Because I know this won't stop any arrows."

...TO REMIND YOU OF YOUR STRENGTH. WHEN YOU ARE READY, PAINT A PICTURE OF YOUR SPECIAL *ANIMAL POWER* ONTO THE SHIELD.

I grabbed a pencil and made an outline of my animal. I tried hard to draw a bear, but it looked more like a big dog.

Maia's shield was perfect, of course. Her crane flew along swirling lines of wind. Antonio painted his bull with red eyes and big horns, jumping through a ring of fire. He held it up proudly.

"Awesome shield, Antonio," I said.

"Thanks. You, too." But I saw him look at Jamie and smile.

"Is this a good eagle?" she asked, showing me her shield. The wings were long, and the body was little. It looked more like a giant moth.

REALLY GOOD.

SET YOUR SHIELDS DOWN TO DRY, AND FOLLOW ME.

Grandmother walked outside onto the ledge and pointed across the land. Two large mountains stood below with a steep valley cutting between them. "The Alley of Arrows leads directly to the Stone Man," she said.

*I don't like the sound of that, either.*

"What do you mean?" asked Maia.

"The valley is very dangerous. If you cannot make it on that trail, there is only one other way to get through," she said.

I gazed over at the tallest, darkest mountain. "In there?" I asked.

IT IS CALLED THE **Mountain of Fear**. IT'S WHERE **HEYOKA** LIVES, AND IT IS THE ONLY OTHER WAY TO THE **STONE MAN**. YOU MUST FOLLOW THE PATHS INSIDE THE MOUNTAIN.

HIS POWER OF **FEAR** AND **HATE** CAN DESTROY MOTHER EARTH.

AS OUR WORLD HAS BECOME MORE SELFISH AND ANGRY, THE **FOUR ELEMENTS** HAVE LOST THEIR BALANCE.

*FIRE, AIR, WATER,* AND *EARTH* MUST ALL BE IN HARMONY IF WE ARE TO SURVIVE. HEYOKA, THE *HATE MASTER*, IS GROWING STRONGER. IT IS UP TO YOU TO HELP RESTORE BALANCE TO OUR WORLD--OR LOVE AND COMPASSION WILL DISAPPEAR. THEN THE *HEARTBEAT* OF MOTHER EARTH WILL STOP FOREVER.

*If I'm afraid now, what will happen to me in there?* I thought. I held my protection pouch tight in my hand.

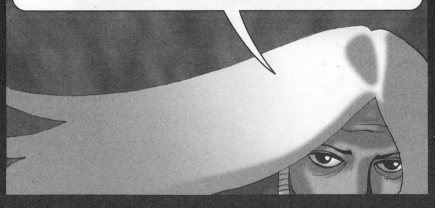

YOU MUST REACH THE STONE MAN BY NIGHTFALL. ONCE YOU DO, YOU WILL GO TO EACH OF THE FOUR DIRECTIONS TO FIND A TALL *STONE MARKER*. YOU MUST PLACE YOUR TOTEM IN THE CORRECT MARKER. ONCE YOUR TOTEMS ARE IN PLACE, HARMONY AND BALANCE CAN BE *RESTORED* TO THE ELEMENTS.

Grandmother saw the confusion in our faces. "Follow me," she said.

She walked inside and went over to a long wooden table. The four totems were lined up in a row. Above the table hung a shield with a picture of a golden palomino horse. It was galloping across a cloud, under a full moon and a rainbow.

Grandmother Dancing Feather held up a fan made of owl feathers. The handle was decorated with colorful glass beads.

MAIA, YOU WILL TAKE THIS TOTEM TO THE EAST OF THE STONE MAN TO CALM THE ELEMENT OF *AIR.*

YES, GRANDMOTHER.

Next, Grandmother picked up the rattles with the red ties.

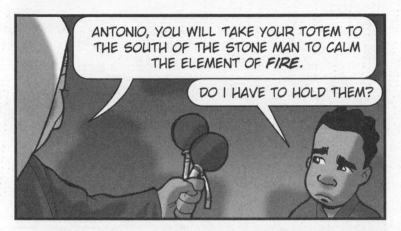

ANTONIO, YOU WILL TAKE YOUR TOTEM TO THE SOUTH OF THE STONE MAN TO CALM THE ELEMENT OF *FIRE.*

DO I HAVE TO HOLD THEM?

Grandmother nodded. He stepped forward, took them carefully in his hands, and bowed.

JUST DON'T *SHAKE* THEM.

Next, Grandmother carried a large black-and-white striped shell over to Jamie.

YOU WILL TAKE THIS TOTEM TO THE WEST OF THE STONE MAN TO CALM THE ELEMENT OF *WATER.*

WITH *HONOR,* GRANDMOTHER.

Now it was my turn. Grandmother held up a clear quartz crystal. It was as big as my hand, and it was pointed at one end.

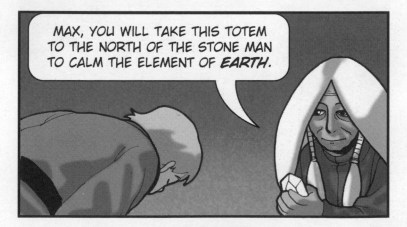

MAX, YOU WILL TAKE THIS TOTEM TO THE NORTH OF THE STONE MAN TO CALM THE ELEMENT OF *EARTH.*

Grandmother then gave each of us a leather storage pack. The packs were filled with food, water, and other supplies for our journey. We were to keep our crystals, totems, and protective pouches inside. Jamie smoothed the special headband her grandmother made for her—she *only* wore it in the dojo and on our missions. We were ready to go.

TIE YOUR PROTECTION SHIELDS ONTO YOUR PACKS.

"Yip-yip-yeow!" A loud coyote howl echoed up the canyon walls.

We looked at each other nervously.

"Time you began your journey. May the four winds guide you and keep you safe!" Grandmother said.

*Uh-oh. I know what that means. Scary things are about to happen.*

# CHAPTER 5

OUR MISSION had begun. We said farewell to Grandmother and left the cliff-house dwelling using a rock-ladder. It was also carved into the side of the mountain. I looked down. Big mistake. It was steep and frightening.

*This must be about twenty stories high!* Everyone was ahead of me, and there was only one way to go — straight down. *This is not good.* I tried to be brave, but after I took a few steps, something happened. I couldn't move. I froze in mid-climb. All I could do was stare at the rock wall in front of me.

"Max!" Antonio yelled up to me.

I looked down at him. The ground began to spin. *I feel funny.*

"Don't look down!" he yelled again.

"Now you tell me!"

I focused on the cliff wall. My heart was beating really fast. *Stay calm. Stay calm.*

"Come on, you can do it!" called Jamie.

They were already at the bottom, and I was still near the top.

I was trying hard to move, but my body wouldn't listen. I was beginning to panic, and my palms were starting to sweat.

Antonio climbed up next to me.

My knuckles had turned white from squeezing the ladder so tightly.

"The one where we breathe in energy and blow out fear. Remember?" he asked.

I followed Antonio with the *ki* breath, and right away I felt less scared. *Inhale, exhale, inhale, exhale.* My head stopped spinning. The fear was slowly leaving me with each breath out.

My grip relaxed a little, and my knuckles looked less white.

Antonio stayed above me on the ladder and let me go down first. "You're cool, Max," he said.

I moved slowly down the ladder until I finally reached the bottom. It was *so* good to be on solid ground again.

Antonio was always so confident. *How does he do that?* I wondered. I looked ahead at the valley in front of us.

"He tried his best, Maia," said Jamie.

Maia glared at me. "Well, we've lost a lot of time."

"So why are we standing here talking?" asked Antonio. "Let's move."

He took the lead as we entered the Alley of Arrows. Even though the sun was still high, criss-crossing shadows folded over the land and made it hard to see the trail. It felt as if someone or something was watching us.

*Heyoka, the Hate Master, could be anywhere!*

# CHAPTER 6

BLACK, JAGGED, steep walls jutted out of the canyon floor and shot high into the sky. The shadows made it seem as if it were already night.

"What are those sharp things sticking out of all the walls?" I asked.

"They look like arrowheads," said Jamie.

"And they're aimed right at us," I added.

"I don't think these shields are going to protect us against those," said Antonio.

"The shields are symbolic. Remember? They're supposed to remind us of our power," said Maia.

"I'd rather have real ones," I said.

"What's real, and what's not, is all a state of mind," said a growling voice.

We jumped into ready stance.

Before us sat a strange creature, crouched atop a tall wall of rock. Its big, curving toes ended in sharp claws, and it had the body of a thick furry man. It smiled widely to reveal razor-sharp teeth inside a gigantic coyote head. Its tongue flicked past its teeth, catching some of the drool that oozed down its chin.

"I'm not afraid of you!" Antonio shouted.

*Speak for yourself,* I thought. *Just looking at that guy makes my stomach ache.*

"Be quiet, Antonio!" I said. Heyoka turned to me.

I felt my face get hot with anger.

"Or are you scared because deep inside you know that even if you called your mommy, she'd never come? And neither would your father!" He growled. "See? I know your deepest secret fear— and so do your friends!"

*I hate him! I hate him!* I thought.

Before I could blink, the Hate Master leaped off his perch and was suddenly crouched behind me. The others jumped into action. Antonio lunged, but before his punch could hit, Heyoka lifted me into the air.

HELP!

Heyoka sprang with his muscular legs. Then he carried me up to his perch.

"Max!" yelled Jamie.

"Let him go, fat head!" shouted Antonio.

Heyoka dropped me next to him. I looked down and caught my breath. We were at least twenty feet above the others. I hate heights, and my head began to spin.

My legs began to shake. *Remember your power, Max. Remember your power,* said a voice in my mind. My bear was trying to help me! *OK, Max, think. You've got to try something, or you're doomed.* I looked again at the Hate Master to see where I could strike him. *If I can target a pressure point, I can get away. I'm already squatting down. If I can shift my weight to my right leg, I can kick his knee out with my left. Here goes.*

I barely moved, but Heyoka instantly grabbed my leg and flipped me onto my back. His giant fangs loomed over my face. My heart was in my throat, and I could hardly breathe.

"Oh boy, you are a lot of fun," he snarled.

"Hey! Heyoka!" yelled Antonio. "How about some fun over here?"

Heyoka growled as he jumped off his perch, right over Antonio's head.

"You're wasting my time," called Heyoka. He was standing behind me again with his claws clinched around my arms. His huge head was above mine, and he was panting. With each gasp, a glob of drool dripped on top of my head. *Disgusting!*

"Your fear charges my battery."

*What? Is he some kind of machine?*

FOR YEARS THE **FOUR ELEMENTS** TRAPPED ME INSIDE THE MOUNTAIN OF FEAR, WITH NO COMPANY BUT THE STONE AROUND ME. I THOUGHT I WOULD GO **CRAZY**, BUT I DIDN'T. INSTEAD, MY ANGER MADE ME **STRONG**.

THEN, ONE DAY, SOME ANIMALS DUG A WAY INTO THE MOUNTAIN TO LOOK FOR WATER. SO I HAD MY FUN WITH THEM. I STOLE THEIR FOOD AND **HUNTED THEM DOWN**.

SOON THEY WERE ALL ENRAGED. THEY BEGAN TO **HATE** ME. JUST AS YOU WILL, TOO.

AND THEY WERE SO AFRAID OF ME THAT THEY CRIED, AND CRIED, AND **CRIED**-- UNTIL ONE DAY, **GUESS WHAT?**

"The animals were crying from fear and hate," I answered.

Heyoka patted me on the back. "See? You could be my assistant."

My teeth began to chatter, so I clamped my mouth shut.

At that, Heyoka let go of me and started to jump. I took a deep breath. I threw a bottom fist strike at his knee, hoping to take him down. But he saw it coming. He sidestepped, and with a blow to my back, he used his big claws to shove me off the ledge. I went tumbling down the jagged hillside.

I could feel Jamie shaking my shoulders, but I couldn't get up. Her voice sounded far, far away. My eyes were closed, and I just wanted to sleep.

Heyoka sprang from the ledge and crouched next to us. "Let me leave you with a thought to remember me by. I know about your childish mission. You'll never make it through the Alley of Arrows, and you'll certainly die in the Mountain of Fear! You're doomed! Yip-yip-yeow!" he howled.

I opened my eyes and watched him run down through the valley. I'm not sure if I was seeing things, but it looked as if the black arrows got a little brighter as he passed.

# CHAPTER 7

HANDS SLID under my arms and lifted me up.

"Huh?" I blinked my eyes and shook my head. "Ouch. I have a killer headache."

"I wonder why," said Maia, letting go of me.

"You did some sweet flips down that hill," said Antonio.

When I looked around, everything seemed kind of fuzzy.

Jamie held a water bottle to my mouth. "Here, drink this."

I took a big gulp, and the world looked normal again. "Thanks."

"Enough delays," said Maia. "We've got to get through this hate-zone by night."

"I'm not going into that mountain!" said Jamie.

We looked down the valley and noticed a crack in the hillside.

The arrows surrounding us grew brighter. *Was it because I used the word "hate"?*

"Why is everyone complaining? You all sound so stupid!" said Maia.

"I can say what I want," snapped Antonio. "You're the stupid one!"

"Hey, guys," said Jamie. "Stop acting like idiots!"

"Well, aren't you Miss Know-It-All," said Maia, making a face.

"Look *away*!" said Jamie.

We closed our eyes and shook our heads.

"Whoa," said Antonio. "I was getting really mad at you guys!"

"This valley is full of hate," said Jamie. "Let's get out of here."

We moved slowly forward, keeping alert. After a few minutes, nothing happened, so we walked a little faster.

STOP! LOOK! THE BLACK ARROWHEADS ARE *BLAZING!*

With his very next step, an arrow whizzed past the tip of Antonio's nose. "Aahh!" he yelled.

We dove to the ground as hundreds of arrows shot out at us all at once.

KEEP YOUR GUARD UP, YOU GUYS, JUST IN CASE.

YOU DON'T HAVE TO TELL ME.

An arrow brushed by my hair. None of us moved another inch. We huddled together on the ground.

I WAS AFRAID THIS WOULD HAPPEN!

"Be quiet, Max!" said Maia. "Fear is what the Hate Master wants!"

I held my pouch tightly in my hand and raised my bear shield.

"OK, let's see if the ball of energy works," said Maia.

We closed our eyes and concentrated on the meditation Grandmother had given us earlier. I imagined energy coming up from the earth into my body. After only a minute, I could feel my hands beginning to tingle. *It's working!* I opened my eyes and saw that we were each surrounded by a ball of light.

WE *DID* IT! LET'S TRY MOVING.

We moved slowly forward. We had made it a few steps when a flurry of arrows shot out at us. We dove back to the ground. One of the arrows hit the wall of light surrounding me. It slowed down, hit my shield, and bounced away. Lucky for me. The arrow had been aimed at my throat.

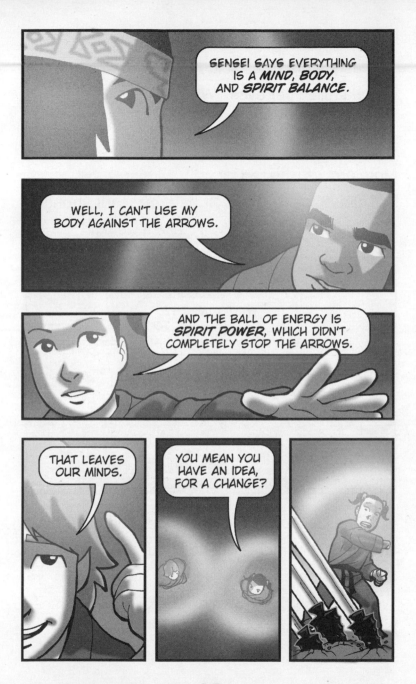

SENSEI SAYS EVERYTHING IS A *MIND, BODY,* AND *SPIRIT BALANCE.*

WELL, I CAN'T USE MY BODY AGAINST THE ARROWS.

AND THE BALL OF ENERGY IS *SPIRIT POWER,* WHICH DIDN'T COMPLETELY STOP THE ARROWS.

THAT LEAVES OUR MINDS.

YOU MEAN YOU HAVE AN IDEA, FOR A CHANGE?

"Nasty is not nice," said Antonio, smiling at her.

Maia rolled her eyes. "Whatever."

"The arrows get brighter when we argue," I said.

"So?" asked Maia, with a mean expression. More arrows whizzed by.

"I get it!" said Jamie. "If hate makes it stronger, then the opposite thing will make it weaker!"

Jamie laughed. Then I laughed. And even Maia laughed. The more we laughed, the duller the arrows became.

"Tell a joke," said Jamie. "Look! Our happiness is taking the power away from the arrows."

We kept telling jokes and laughing. We told the silliest stories we could think up. Slowly we inched our way along the valley floor.

"Keep going, you guys. We're almost halfway through the valley," said Maia.

We made it to the small opening in the mountain wall. It looked terrifying. *I'm not going there. No way!* And with my fearful thought, arrows whizzed by me again.

"Run for cover!" yelled Antonio. All of them scrambled into the cave.

"Not in there!" I yelled. "Wait!"

Arrows whizzed dangerously close to my head. I rolled and skipped, trying to dodge them as I headed for the cave. I dove through the opening just in time!

# CHAPTER 8

FEAR WAS thick in the air. My stomach twisted into a knot. The cave was dark and we were tired from the arrow attack. I reached into my pack and pulled out a flashlight. I aimed it at the wall and the ceiling.

"Whoa! This cave is huge!" I said.

"I can't even see the top," said Jamie.

"Cool graffiti!" said Antonio, pointing his light onto a large wall mural.

"I learned about those in school," said Jamie. "They're pictographs—really old paintings that tell a story."

"Maybe we can get some clues about how to get to the Stone Man from here," I said.

The wall art showed faded pictures of different animals drinking.

Around the corner was a small, round lake. Thick salt-rock spires pointed down from the high ceiling.

*The darkness of this place is making me sad.*

We walked to the right side of the lake and found three tunnels going in different directions.

"Now what?" I asked.

Antonio aimed his flashlight down the largest tunnel. "I think the sound's coming from in there," he said.

We stood under a large stone canopy, near the entrance to the three tunnels. Eight pillars, four on each side, held up a large dome overhead. I leaned against one of the stone pillars, and something poked me in the back. I turned around and rubbed my hand across the column.

"Jamie, does this look like hair to you?" I asked.

She rubbed her hand on it and jumped away. "Ew! What is it?"

ARE YOU SURE THIS IS THE RIGHT TUNNEL?

I DON'T KNOW, BUT THE *MOANING* SOUND IS LOUDEST IN THERE.

HEY, GUYS, THERE'S SOMETHING *WEIRD* OVER THERE.

SCREEEEECH!!!

A screeching noise boomed through the cavern as the eight pillars began to move!

"Aahh!"

The ground rumbled and knocked us off our feet. We looked up and couldn't believe our eyes. Hovering above us was a giant . . .

Antonio shuffled to the right, and a hairy leg followed his every move. He tried to roll, but a leg thumped the dirt next to him. He threw a counter punch, but it didn't make a dent. Another leg jabbed at Maia. She shuffled backward until she was against the cave wall with nowhere to go. A pile of boulders were stacked up next to her. I could tell they were slightly off balance.

"Maia! Kick the rocks!" I yelled.

She looked at me and tripped over a stone. The spider leg rose in the air and was about to stomp on Maia when she saw the stack of rocks.

TAKE THAT, YOU NASTY ARACHNID!

"Yahoo!" I shouted.

I wasn't looking behind myself when another prickly leg snuck up on me and swept me off my feet. The huge body zoomed toward my face. I was suddenly eye-to-eye with an ugly alien-like tarantula that had black, snapping prongs for lips.

"Max!" Antonio and Jamie ran and jumped to strike the monster from opposite directions. But its free legs lashed out and knocked them out of the air. The tarantula reared up and screeched. The sound was deafening.

"Let's get out of here!" yelled Maia.

We took off sprinting. The monster spider stabbed at the ground, trying to attack us as we ran.

Jamie and I got away just in time. We hid inside a small tunnel. The spider poked its hairy leg through the opening, feeling around inside.

The tarantula's leg suddenly pulled away. It was too quiet.

"I hope Maia and Antonio are OK!" Jamie said.

Suddenly the spider squealed.

"No! Get off me!" Maia was screaming.

Jamie and I looked at each other. "We've got to go help them!" she said.

I tiptoed back into the main cavern just as Maia blasted by. She almost knocked us off our feet.

Bats zipped back and forth! They were attacking us *and* the tarantula!

"Those are some kind of weird, mutant vampire bats!" I yelled. A flurry of wings flicked at my head.

"Run for the lake!" called Maia.

She ran as fast as she could, but it wasn't fast enough. A dozen huge, aggressive vampire bats scooped her up and lifted her into the air. She punched at them to knock them away, but their grip was too tight.

LET ME GO, YOU SMELLY *BLOOD SUCKERS!*

Suddenly, a cloud of bats grabbed Jamie.

"Give me a lift!" Antonio yelled. He jumped onto my shoulders and sprang into the air. He struck at the bats with twelve super-speed double kicks, right into their bellies.

They squeaked and dropped Jamie. But a second cluster of bats caught her midair. They didn't stop coming. They dove at us in a crisscross pattern, making it hard for us to take aim. Their wings stung my cheeks. Antonio and I picked up the pace. We kicked and punched at lightning speed so they couldn't get a grip on us. Finally, they whipped around and flew off.

"They're headed for the lake!" I yelled.

We climbed up to a higher ledge.

WHEN THOSE BATS FLY BY US, JUMP AND *GRAB* MAIA! I'LL GET JAMIE.

BUT THAT'S A LONG WAY DOWN! WHAT IF I MISS? AND HOW AM I SUPPOSED TO...

*GET READY!* THEY'RE ALMOST HERE!

The bats carrying Jamie were right next to us.

Antonio sprang from the ledge and grabbed her feet. Now they were *both* dangling in the air! The bats made an angry noise as Jamie and Antonio hit them hard. Then the bats lost their grip and dropped Jamie and Antonio into the water.

Now Maia was almost in reach.

*Come on, Max. You can do it. You've got to jump. It's now or never!* I bent my knees and took a deep breath. *If I miss,* I thought, *it's a long way down. And I might not even hit the water, which means I'm dead!* I bit my lip. Maia went swinging past me.

"Max! Do something!" she yelled.

But it was too late. The bats whizzed by and were over the lake before I could jump.

They let her go.

"No!" she screamed. But of course Maia was Maia, so she made the most of her fall. On her way down, she performed a double somersault and entered the water with a perfect jackknife dive.

I stood shivering on the ledge. Across the cave, the monster tarantula had spun an enormous web.

*Phew, I think I'm safe.* But just as I was about to climb down from the ledge, a new flurry of bats dove at me! I jumped up and did a split kick.

"The vampires are back! Jump!" yelled Jamie.

I looked down at the lake. "No way!"

A bat landed on my neck and tried to attack me. I threw a quick hook punch and sent it tumbling down the rocks.

Another one whipped past my head and yanked at my hair.

"Ouch! *Kiai!*"

I threw a sword-hand strike and hit it right under its wing. It screeched and darted away. But a new squad of bats was headed toward me. *I've got to get out of here! There are too many of them! It's now or never!*

With a leap of faith, I jumped off the ledge. But I didn't dive with the grace of a crane, the way Maia did. My power is the bear, and I fell hard—like a big fat one.

A strong current was pulling us to the other side of the lake. The rushing water was getting louder. We saw a small opening in the wall and realized we were about to get sucked right into it!

"Swim!" yelled Maia.

I kicked my legs, trying to swim away from the hole in the wall. But the current was too strong. *I don't want to drown,* I thought. The water became rougher and splashed into my mouth. I coughed.

"Stay together!" called Maia. "And keep your heads up!"

*Swoosh! Thurp-slurp! Splash!* One at a time we were sucked through the opening, and into the darkness!

# CHAPTER 9

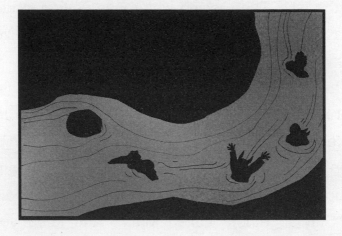

SCREAMS ECHOED off the walls as we went shooting down a dark, watery tunnel. The stream moaned and gurgled with strange, sad noises. I began to feel sad myself. *Will I be trapped in here forever? Doomed to an underground existence of pain and fear? Alone. I'm all alone. No one will even know I'm gone.* With a sudden *swoosh* I slid down a waterfall.

"Aahh!"

*Splash!* I hit the bottom and rose back up to the surface. I landed in a small, dark pool. The light was low, so I could barely see.

"Guys? Are you here?" All I heard was the sound of rushing water. "Antonio? Jamie? Maia?"

Silence. *Did I lose my friends? Friends— I guess they're my friends. I mean, we don't get together and play or anything, and none of them ever calls me. We just see one another at the dojo. Does that mean we're friends?*

I floated on my back to catch my breath. The current was still pulling me. I flipped over onto my stomach and swam as hard as I could toward the shore. A light flicked across my eyes.

MAX! OVER HERE! IT'S ME--ANTONIO!

I paddled hard and let Antonio grab me.

"Awesome waterslide, huh, Max?" Antonio was grinning.

"Yeah, sure," I said, coughing more water out of my throat. "Awesome."

But Maia couldn't speak. She could only cry. And it was getting louder and louder and . . .

Antonio sniffled. "Hey, man, what are you looking at?"

Tears rolled down his cheeks. He used his sleeve to wipe them away, but tears kept coming. Suddenly Jamie was crying, too!

*Oh great! I'm next, and I'll never hear the end of it.* I waited for the tears to come, but still nothing happened. Not one drop.

MAX, YOU'RE NOT CRYING! TRY AND HELP US! SOMEHOW THE STREAM IS MAKING THE REST OF US CRY.

WHAT SHOULD I DO?

She couldn't answer because now she and Maia were weeping and wailing. They looked like two little babies, kicking the ground. *Where is my camera when I need it?*

I looked around the cave and noticed another small opening in the side wall. *Well, at least it's on dry land. I hope it's a way out, but knowing my luck, we'll end up trapped in this mountain forever.* Everyone was crying so hard, they were doubled over in pain. *Why wasn't I crying, too? Maybe I was just used to crying, or to holding my tears inside.*

I aimed my flashlight into the small tunnel. It was dark, and that meant no light was coming from the outside. *Bad sign number one.* Also, the tunnel seemed to drop downward, much deeper into the mountain. *Bad sign number two. Maybe we shouldn't go in there.*

"Ouch! Hey, wait!" My friends were pushing past me. They stumbled into the darkness. "Wait!" I yelled again.

*Great, just great. I couldn't see them, but I could still hear them crying. This isn't fair. Even when I'm the leader, I'm still not the leader.*

*I'm alone again.* I was finally about to cry myself when a voice popped into my head. *Max,* it said, *always remember—there is nothing to fear but fear itself.* Sensei had told me those words again and again. Now I thought I was beginning to understand what she meant.

*Easier said than done!* And with my next step, my feet went out from under me. I was sliding down another slippery slope!

*Splash!* Suddenly I was underwater. I doggie-paddled as fast as I could to get to the surface. I gasped and coughed for air. I rubbed my eyes, but I could hardly see anything.

The cave was quiet, and I was all alone. A little light shone in from the far side. It lit up the wall just enough for me to see cave paintings. But these were different. This time, Heyoka was painted on the wall. In fact, it looked as if he were popping *out* of the wall—as if he had been born out of the mountain. In another picture, he was surrounded by animals, but they didn't look friendly. Their eyes were blood-red, and they were clawing and biting one another.

Crouched next to the wall, so close I could smell him, was the Hate Master!

I paddled frantically toward the opposite side of the cave. Heyoka sprang and landed right next to my hand as I reached the shore. He grabbed my arm and jerked me out of the water. I shivered. My body was stiff from the cold. I put my right foot back into ready stance.

Quicker than I could blink, he leaped as if he had springs in his legs. I moved into action.

I shuffled sideways and did a pivoting back kick. But he was too fast. His howl hurt my ears.

"You think a bully like you can stop *us*?" I shouted. *What am I saying? I'm all alone here.*

His evil eyes grew bright. "That's right. Show me your anger and fear!"

"No! Get away from me!" I stepped back slowly, but with each step I took, he took one, too.

He sprang at me. I dropped to one knee and did a
spinning mule kick. But as my leg whipped around,
Heyoka grabbed it.

He was dragging me away. Suddenly, out of nowhere, Antonio flew in with a loud scream. "*Kiai!* Take this, you nasty hound dog!"

Heyoka turned, and Antonio's flying side kick landed squarely on his nose. "Ah-oo! Yip-yip-yeow!" Heyoka howled.

Jamie and Maia came up behind him with a fast kick-punch combination that had the Hate Master tumbling forward.

He flipped over and then sprang to his feet with a vicious growl. "You may have won this round, but you'll never make it out of this cave alive!" he roared. Then he bounded away through a crack in the side wall.

"Let's follow him!" yelled Antonio. "He knows the way out!"

We squeezed through the opening and chased the monster of hate through the darkness.

# CHAPTER 10

WALLS OF stone pressed on both sides of me. The tunnel was so narrow that I kept scraping my elbows as I ran. I could barely see anything, and it was getting harder to squeeze my body through the passageway. Just when I thought I couldn't move, the top of the narrow canyon opened up to the sky. Light filled the space and lit up the curved layers of sandstone. The walls looked like waves of stone rippling out in all different colors.

"Max! Where are you?"

"Here!" I called. My voice echoed up to the sky.

"Keep walking to the left!" shouted Antonio.

I turned and twisted, but I was careful to always keep my hand on the left wall. The sky above me grew stormy. A gust of wind almost knocked me off my feet. I grabbed at the smooth wall, but now there was nothing to hold on to. *What's happening outside?* The cave shook violently, and a flash of lightning blinded me for a second.

"Hurry, Max. Run!" yelled Maia.

I moved as fast as I could, but the wind was pushing against me. Finally, the passage opened up to an overlook near the top of the mountain.

From high above, we looked down in amazement. Below us, on the ground, a pile of boulders formed a huge outline of a person.

"That must be the Stone Man!" shouted Maia, above the roar of the wind.

"Nature is going crazy all around it!" I said.

Far below, at the Stone Man's feet, a volcano erupted. Hot, fiery lava shot into the air.

On the right side, a tornado whipped madly. The twister was out of control. It was tearing up trees and plants and spitting them out like pebbles.

An earthquake rumbled at the head of the Stone Man, and the land rippled, rolled, and cracked open. And on the left side, an enormous tidal wave rose and fell, over and over in one spot, washing away everything in its path.

I could see that the dangerous elements were growing stronger by the minute.

"Watch out!" I yelled.

A mangled cactus flew by us. We dodged it just in time.

"And the earth in the north would flatten me like a pancake!" I said.

A gust of wind whipped my *gi*. It felt as if cold hands were trying to strip away my clothes. It was almost dark, and no one knew what to do.

The wind was wild, and we could barely hear one another. The volcano lit up the sunset sky. The mountain we sat upon rumbled with a loud *crack*! *Boom! Think about the clues, Max. Think! Think!*

Sand and dust stung my eyes. The shield on my back began to shake as if it were going to rip off and blow away. *The shield! That's it!* I reached around and untied it.

We sat in a circle, each of us in our direction of power. We held our shields in our laps.

"Now what?" I asked.

"This was *your* idea!" said Maia.

*OK,* I thought, *what did Grandmother say again?* My mind was blank. All I could think about was the danger all around us. Here we were, alone on top of this dark mountain, in the middle of the night, in the middle of nowhere! The world was full of anger and fear, and I could feel it getting stronger inside me, too. I closed my eyes to pray. *Grandmother, we need your help. I wish you were here!*

"Uh, guys?" said Antonio.

I rubbed my eyes, trying to focus against the wind. Between the swirling clouds of dust, I barely made out the shape of a horse. It was galloping up the zigzag mountain trail. A red cape spiraled around the horse and rider.

Grandmother rode to the top of the mountain. Her long hair blew in the wind, and her eyes glowed bright with power.

134

She turned suddenly and rode away. Her cape whipped in the wind as the horse galloped back down the mountain. With a burst of lightning from above, she vanished into the dark night.

The four elements below erupted into even greater chaos. The volcano exploded so strongly that a red-hot chunk of lava shot out and landed right in the middle of our circle.

We scrambled backward. The lava rock broke apart, and warm flames burned brightly in front of us.

"Instant campfire!" said Antonio.

We held out our hands to warm them. The night air was so cold, and the fire felt good.

137

A blast of wind lifted us into the air and threw us dangerously close to the cliff's edge. My fingers dug into the dirt to stop myself from falling off the mountain. Below, Heyoka stood in the middle of the Stone Man. He waved his arms as if he were conducting music.

As he turned to the south, the volcano erupted.

Then he lifted his arm to the east. The tornado
spun faster.

He flashed his teeth to the north, and the earth growled. Giant boulders smashed together.

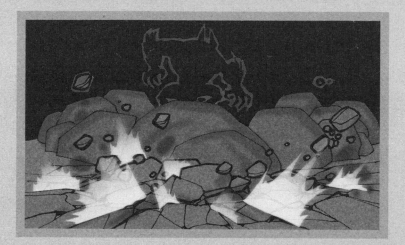

Then he twisted his body west, and the tidal wave crashed down upon itself and grew even taller. He looked up and saw us lying next to the edge of the cliff.

Vicious, snarling animals came out from behind the rocks and circled him as he conducted the four elements in wild music that only he could hear. Heyoka dangled a piece of meat in front of them. They snapped wickedly, trying to get it. He laughed and threw the meat to the ground. They pounced, clawed, and chewed at one another, fighting to the death just for a taste. Heyoka howled with delight and held up his arms.

I held my shield up against the wind. I closed my eyes and focused on my Animal Power, feeling it coming into my body.

My bear approached quickly. In my mind, I saw him running to me from the Alley of Arrows. He was fast and swift and dodged the arrows that shot at him. He bounded up the mountain, and then I felt a jolt as his spirit entered my body.

Suddenly, my muscles felt stronger. I opened my eyes and saw Maia, Jamie, and Antonio standing tall against the wind. They, too, had their Animal Powers within them. *If we have any chance at all, it's now!*

146

I was standing strong with my shield held high.
All of them looked at me.

The four elements were blazing out of control.
The wind was about to knock us off the mountain.
The world was coming to an end, and I couldn't think
of one thing that made me happy — *really* happy.
I mean, I like karate, but Jamie already said that. I
looked over at the three karate kids holding their

shields to the wind. We were a team. We worked together to face danger and fear. We shared ideas and learned things from one another. We could always depend on help if we needed it. Suddenly I thought of something that made me happy. But it wasn't a *thing*—it was more like a feeling.

I held my shield up to the wind and shouted as loud as I could:

As soon as I yelled, the dark clouds above split open. With a burst of light, a giant rainbow bridge arched across the Stone Man. Everything lit up, as if it were morning.

AWESOME! MAX!
*YOU DID IT!*

"Friends! Friends! Friends!" we shouted all together, looking down at the Hate Master.

Heyoka screamed and howled in horror at the sight of the rainbow bridge and the brilliant light.

Then something amazing happened. I heard the sound of drumbeats booming with the loudest thunder I've ever heard!

LISTEN. IT'S THE *HEARTBEAT* OF MOTHER EARTH!

BOOM-BOOM! BOOM-BOOM! BOOM-BOOM! BOOM-BOOM! BOOM-BOOM! BOOM-BOOM!

The animals below moaned and spun frantically in circles. Wild dogs scratched at their own ears as if they were trying to take the sound away. Snakes hissed and twisted themselves into knots.

Owls and hawks flapped their wings on the dirt, trying to take flight. Prairie dogs popped in and out of holes, looking for a place to hide.

But the drumming continued. And the pounding grew louder and louder! Suddenly, all the animals fell at once to the ground and lay perfectly still. The Hate Master looked up. His eyes were full of fear and anguish.

A hawk fluttered its large wings and sent out a piercing screech. It lifted off the ground and flew away. The other animals awoke. They ran and slithered and scurried as fast as they could, far away from Heyoka. Once-vicious wild dogs and coyotes leaped to their feet. They raced off together in a pack, wagging their tails.

Heyoka's yelp became a growl that changed into a whimper. He held his massive head with his claws and sank to the ground.

"Whoa!" said Antonio. "He's transforming!"

The drumbeat of Mother Earth overpowered Heyoka's mind.

IT LOOKS LIKE HE'S GOING TO EXPLODE!

With a painful howl, Heyoka shriveled and shrank into a sniveling, puny coyote. He ran out of the Stone Man and back into the mountain with his tail between his legs.

The drumbeats came harder and faster. With a loud *boom*, rocks burst from all sides of the mountain.

"Avalanche!" yelled Antonio. "Watch out!"

A river of stones and boulders rolled past us.

We jumped out of the way just in time.

Any openings in or out of the mountain were sealed. Heyoka, the Hate Master, was now trapped forever inside his own Mountain of Fear.

In the east, the wild tornado had turned into a small breeze. It gently blew across some newly sprouted wildflowers.

LOOK AT THE WEST. THE TIDAL WAVE HAS BECOME A BEAUTIFUL POND. I CAN EVEN SEE FISH JUMPING!

THE VOLCANO IS NOTHING BUT A LITTLE CAMPFIRE NOW. WHO WANTS TO ROAST SOME MARSHMALLOWS?

IT ALMOST LOOKS AS IF THE FLOWERS ARE WAVING HELLO.

I looked to the north, the place of earth. It was quiet. No more earthquakes, and no more fear. The cactus and rocks spread across the land as if they were in a park where people could go to relax. *Just like I want to do right now.* The drumbeat of Mother Earth faded. The sky cleared, and in the east, the sun was rising. Golden light filled the circle.

The rainbow bridge rose up into the sky and faded into the clouds.

*The world is safe,* I thought. *We are not going to die from hate and fear, because friendship and laughter conquered the Hate Master.*

We zigzagged down the mountainside onto the plain below. We each walked around the Stone Man to place our totems in the markers. I stood in the north and reached into my pack. I pulled out the clear quartz crystal that Grandmother Dancing Feather had given me.

The stone marker was tall, and I had to stand on a rock to reach it. I placed the crystal into the marker. The morning light shone through the stone, and a rainbow prism lit it up inside.

Antonio put his rattles in the south, Jamie placed her shell in the west, while Maia set her fan in the east. We walked to the middle of the Stone Man, where the Hate Master had just finished his last symphony.

IT FEELS GOOD HERE. AS IF NOTHING EVER HAPPENED. THIS PROVES THAT LOVE IS STRONGER THAN HATE.

A slight breeze blew through our hair. The birds were singing, the sun was shining, and the sky was bright blue.

Antonio and I looked at each other. I lifted my hand to join Jamie's, but Antonio stopped me. "Hey, just because we're friends it doesn't mean we have to act all lovey-dovey," he said.

"Uh, yeah," I said, tucking my hand into my belt.

"Fine with me," said Maia.

We formed a circle at the heart of the Stone Man and began the Four Winds Kata. The land around me was peaceful. The sun shone onto the lake where birds now drank from fresh water. The green grass under my feet felt like a soft bed calling out for me to take a nap. A breeze was warm on my cheeks. I don't know why, but I thought about my mother. She left when I was little. I don't really remember her, but I can imagine her next to me sometimes. Usually when I think about her I feel sad. But for the first time in a long time, the thought of her made me feel good.

We moved faster now. All around us, fire, air, water, and earth were in perfect balance. I knew it was time to go home.

# CHAPTER 11

WE WERE still moving fast when we landed in the dojo. We slowed down, and then we stopped.

"Welcome home," said Sensei. "Line up."

"*Osu*, Sensei." We moved quickly to the line for our final bow to show respect to one another before leaving the dojo.

Sensei walked over to a side table and pulled something out of a drawer. "You should all be proud of yourselves. You have once again proven that you are true champions. Because of your courage and focus, you have helped another world regain its harmony and balance."

From inside her sleeve, she pulled out a large patch. "Today, one of you in particular has passed all the requirements needed to earn his animal patch. He trusted his inner strength to guide him through his fears. He tried his best, and he never gave up."

The others were looking at me. I felt a smile creeping across my face.

MAX, STEP FORWARD, PLEASE.

THANK YOU, *SENSEI.*

Everyone clapped for me. I was happy and excited and proud all at once.

Everyone's parents were waiting outside for them. I looked down the street, but Uncle Al was nowhere in sight. I began to walk to the bus when he pulled up beside me.

"Don't expect *me* to sew It on," he sald. He punched the radio and blasted the news.

As we drove home, I stared out the window in the backseat, and I felt really happy. I wasn't thinking about the great battle we had just won, or the fun karate moves I like to do, or going home and playing with Lucy. I wasn't even thinking about the cool patch I was holding in my hands. All I could think about right now was one thing, and one thing only: friends. There was nothing better in the whole wide world than having friends!

# BASIC KARATE TECHNIQUES

When Max Greene was training for his black belt, he practiced these karate moves. Be sure an adult is present to help you. And remember: The karate you learn here is only used for self-defense, and only when there is no other option.

**jab/reverse strike**

**back knuckle strike**

# hook kick

# forward shoulder roll

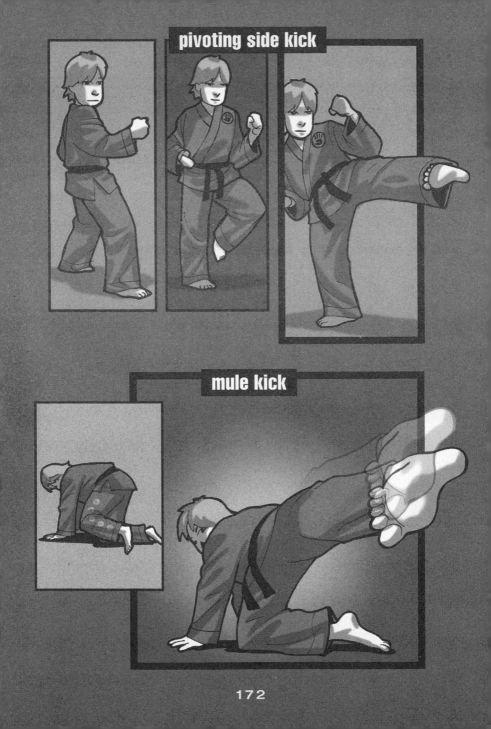

pivoting side kick

mule kick

**jumping side kick**

**hopping front kick**

173

## ABOUT THIS BOOK

KARATE IS a type of martial art where a student learns physical and mental discipline for balance of mind, body, and spirit. It is believed that martial arts were created several thousand years ago in China by Shaolin monks who needed a way to protect themselves from traveling warlords. Over time, martial arts evolved into hundreds of different styles that spread throughout the Far East. Some of the moves practiced in this book are based upon Shotokan karate techniques from Japan. The word karate means "empty hand," because we learn how to protect ourselves without using weapons.

Many of the teachings and concepts in this book are an extension of my personal studies with two highly respected Shamans, or Medicine People. Grandmother Twylah Nitsch of the Seneca Nation initiated me into the Wolf Clan and taught me the value of "walking in beauty within the Circle of Power." Joseph Rael, Beautiful Painted Arrow of the Ute tribe, taught me the importance of seeing the whole picture—honoring "all my relations," whether they be the four-legged ones, the two-legged ones, the stone people, the tree people, or the winged ones. He taught me that every entity on this planet has a special "sound" through which we may connect to a greater force. In this book, I have tried to pass along some of these ancient teachings so that our children may begin to understand the idea of interconnectedness between themselves and other living beings.

Karate is a great way to get in shape, to gain confidence,

and to have fun! To learn more, check your library, the Internet, or www.theblackbeltclub.com.

DAWN BARNES is a third-degree black belt and the founder of Dawn Barnes Karate Kids, the most successful all-children's karate school in the U.S. As well, she is the Director of Children's Education for the National Association of Professional Martial Artists. She lives in Los Angeles. BERNARD CHANG began his career in the comic book world, where his work on such popular characters as Doctor Mirage, Superman, and the X-Men earned him a coveted spot on the top ten artists in *Wizard: The Guide to Comics*. He lives in Los Angeles.

## SOME KARATE TERMS

| WORD | PRONUNCIATION | MEANING |
| --- | --- | --- |
| dojo | doe-joh | karate school |
| gi | gee | karate uniform |
| ki | kee | spirit |
| kiai | kee-eye | spirit power |
| sensei | sen-say | karate teacher |
| osu | oss | yes, I understand |
| kiotsuki, rei | kee-o-skay, ray | attention, bow |

## FOR MORE KARATE MOVES...

read *The Black Belt Club: Seven Wheels of Power*. In that book, you will see the following: upward block, x-block, inward block, downward block, front kick, side kick, back kick, straight punch, palmheel strike, hammerfist strike, roundhouse kick, and wheel kick.